THE Talkative Tortoise

Andrew Fusek Peters   illustrated by Charlotte Cooke

Child's Play (International) Ltd

Ashworth Rd, Bridgemead, Swindon SN5 7YD, UK

Swindon   Auburn ME   Sydney

ISBN 978-1-84643-586-7   L220119CPL04195867

Text © 2011 Andrew Fusek Peters Illustration © 2011 Child's Play (International) Ltd

Printed in Heshan, China

7 9 10 8 6

www.childs-play.com

One day, Tortoise crawled to the edge
of the lake to have a wash, a drink
and a chat. At the water's edge, he met
his two best friends – a pair of geese.

Tortoise was lucky, because geese are known
to be extremely good listeners,
and Tortoise could talk like nobody's business.

"Do you think it's easy to keep
my shell as shiny and smooth as this?"
he asked as he waded into the lake.

"Of course not,"
one of the geese replied.

"I have to wash my shell all over
with the finest lake water and
then shine it with the softest moss
I can find!" said Tortoise,
splashing about in the cool water.

The geese nodded their heads
and gave a little quack or two.
They'd heard the story a hundred times.

One day, as the first snow fell
on the far mountains, the geese decided
it was time to fly south.
"It will be winter soon," said one.
"We need to fly to our feeding grounds."

Tortoise began to cry.
"But you can't leave me behind.
I'll be so lonely! Who will I talk to?
Who will I play with?
And who will look after me?"
he wailed.

"Sorry!" said the other goose. "Yak and sheep will keep you company. But we have to leave."

Tortoise had a huge tantrum.
He sobbed. He sighed,
"Oh! Oh! Oh!
It's not fair! Can't I come too?"

"But you can't fly!"
said one of the geese.

"Carry me, carry me!"
replied Tortoise.

"We can't carry you. Your shell is too smooth.
It would slip out of our beaks!" said the other goose.

"Please! Please! Pretty please!" begged Tortoise,
as the tears rolled down his scaly cheeks.

The geese discussed the problem and soon
came up with a solution. One of them
waddled off into a bush and came back
dragging a long, sturdy stick.

"We will lift both ends, and you must bite
on the middle with your strong jaw!" said the first goose.

"And hold on tight!" said the second.
"Which means," they both warned,
"you mustn't talk the whole time we are flying!"

Tortoise smiled. His two best friends had come to the rescue!

"Oh, that's easy.
I can stay quiet for seconds,
minutes, hours, days, weeks,
months, seasons, years…"

"We get the point, Tortoise!"
said the first goose.
"You'd better do as we say!"
warned the second goose.

The very next morning, the wind was light
and the sky was as clear as crystal.
The two geese clamped each end of the stick
in their beaks and asked Tortoise to hold on.

He crawled up to the middle of the stick, opened his mouth as wide as he could and bit down hard.

The geese flapped their wings, struggling with the extra weight, but within seconds they were rising into the air.

Tortoise was true to his word, keeping his mouth firmly shut and closing his eyes in terror!

When he finally opened his eyes,
Tortoise saw that the geese
had flown high above the lake
and the plain. He was fascinated.

He could see sheep, goats, yurts and people.
He wanted to tell his good friends all about it,
but remembered to stay quiet just in time.

They flew over rolling plains
dotted with villages, rivers filled
with houseboats and boats
carrying vegetables to market.

Soon, the air grew cold as they climbed towards the mountains. Tortoise was desperate to tell his good friends all about it, but he remembered to stay quiet just in time.

They soared over the mountain tops
and down into India.
Soon, they left the snow behind
and there were lush green forests below.

In time, his friends flew over a village.
People looked up and shouted,
"Look! Two geese carrying a tortoise!"

Tortoise was annoyed.
He wanted to say to the geese,
"They should mind
their own business!"
But he managed just in time
to remember his promise
to keep his lips zipped tight.

Tortoise loved the feeling of flying. The wind brushed his shell, giving it even more of a polish, while his eyes feasted on the wonderful sights and sounds of the miniature world below. There was so much he wanted to tell the geese, but it would have to wait until they landed.

As the sun began to set, they flew over a town.
The people there looked up and laughed,

"Amazing!
Have you ever seen anything so funny?
It's a flying tortoise!"

Tortoise was so angry.
The people should have been impressed
by how clever he was to hitch a ride
with his two best friends! His lips twitched,
his teeth clattered together and his tongue
began to dance inside his mouth.

As the townspeople
far below burst into
giggles, their laughter
spread like ripples
across a pond.

Tortoise could hold back no longer.

"Oh, do be quiet
you silly bunch of FOOLS!"

OOOPS!

Tortoise realized his mistake too late.
He'd opened his mouth! He didn't even
have time to say goodbye to his friends.

Instead, he fell like a big shiny stone
straight
down
to
the
ground.

Tortoise landed with a huge bump, bounced
twice and rolled over rocks and soil
until finally he came to a rest.
His once smooth and shiny shell
was now cracked and rough all over.
As it is to this day!

CRASH!

BANG!

THUMP!

So if you ever try talking to a tortoise,
he won't give an answer. No way!

He's finally learned his lesson.
Now he knows, as we all should,
when to keep his big mouth shut!